The Legend of Roaring Gorge

Ronald Gaines

ISBN: 978-0578179704

Papaw Publications USA
www.papawpublications.com

Roaring River Falls at the Upper End of the Gorge

INTRODUCTION

Many Americans aren't familiar with the Cohutta Wilderness. For those of you who may not know, its 40,000 acres extend from the northeastern corner of Georgia into the southeastern corner of Tennessee, where it's known as the Big Frog Wilderness Area.

The Cohutta is home to the beautiful and often mysterious-looking Great Smoky Mountains – a subrange of the larger and longer Appalachian chain.

As settlers moved west, most chose to avoid the area due to little flat land for farming and overall difficultly of access. But a number of families accepted the challenge of scratching out a living in the area.

There are unnumbered stories about early mountain life in the southeastern United States, the majority *about* people in the Cohutta. But there were stories shared *among* the settlers that are equally interesting.

One began almost 150 years ago. The telling and retelling has served to heighten intrigue far beyond any requisite for detailed authentication.

As you can judge from the length of this book, the story doesn't take long to tell.

In the main, I've chosen to use simple narrative, sharing details repeated by purveyors of the grand oral tradition. In other places, however, I've taken the liberty of fleshing out details by lending voice and emotion to those who lived the legend.

In addition, I've tried to make it a quick and easy read. Hopefully, I succeeded.

So let's spend a little time together sharing *The Legend of Roaring Gorge*.

Contents

One

Unintended Consequences

The disease in Felton Baggett's body was worsening. Dizziness and nausea were constant companions. He couldn't see as well as he could only three months earlier, and the simplest of tasks were increasingly difficult – those such as holding the heavy musket steady long enough to guarantee accuracy at 100 yards across the northern end of the Gorge.

Baggett had considered the shot for weeks and planned it for days. The ailing and

Early March, 1878

embittered leader of the Baggett clan was committed to making the week at hand the last his neighbor would live.

The Legend of Roaring Gorge Gaines

As was so often the case in those days, the feud between the mountain families wasn't over politics or other public matters. It was rooted in something more private and far more personal – something second only to family – land.

oooo

In the fall of 1877, after weeks of bitter wrangling and deep anger, a judge ruled in favor of Nelson Vandable, and rights to 20-acres long worked by the Baggetts were awarded to the Vandable estate.

Felton Baggett's reaction was deeply bitter and no less spiteful. Rather than soothing inflamed emotions, the intervening months only heightened his rage and deepened his depression.

The Legend of Roaring Gorge Gaines

Just after dawn on that portentous day, the North Georgia mountain air was heavy. It always felt that way at the northern, shallower end of the Gorge where moisture from the falls clung to ravine's steep, craggy walls before spilling over its ragged edge.

oooo

The previous five days had been unusually cold, and the Vandable wood shed was nearing empty. Hollis, Nelson's oldest child, was stacking wedges as his father struggled to split the hardwood rounds.

"Boy, how many times I gotta tell you and your sisters to cut these rounds shorter? When the wood's this knotty, the rounds gotta be shorter than this," blustered Nelson Vandable, while pointing to the five remaining pieces of oak.

"Don't ya know, the longer the round, the harder it is to split?" asked Vandable, stopping just short of showing real anger. Hollis' father knew well his son's limitations and always tried to take that into consideration when correcting the boy.

"I-I-I know Paw, but lots of this wuz sawed by 'becca and Bonnie, while I wuz mi-mi-milkin' the cows," replied the boy in his familiar, halting manner.

For the most part, Hollis understood and was able to deal with routines around the Vandable household. But it was the unexpected, the loud, seemingly intrusive experiences from time to time that frightened and disoriented him. When he was in his early teens, dynamite used to clear rocks for a road near his home sent Hollis into nearby woods where he hid for the better part of two days.

For the 19-year-old, difficulty resolving internal conflict and moderating stress had always run deeper and taken longer than what might be expected from children of sounder mind.

His efforts in the one-room school house fell short of the norm. What little structured education he had was the result of his mother's nightly efforts around the kerosene lantern.

His physical appearance only added to the unease many felt in his presence. Dark, coarse hair not only grew in random directions on his head, it grew in similar fashion on his arms, legs and much of his torso. Even the tops of his fingers and backs of his hands showed excessive hair growth.

His large stature, deep voice and exaggerated laugh, as well as a tendency to peer out from under his often-lowered eyebrows combined to make him look all the more oafish – and, to many, all the more frightening.

In sharp contrast, Nelson and Charlotte's identical twin daughters, Rebecca and Bonnie, were the polar opposite of their older brother. The fifteen-year-old girls were fair-complected, gracious in their manner and the envy of every young man in Bounds County.

In truth, both girls loved Hollis deeply and sought to help their parents deal with the challenges he brought into the family. As the twins had grown older, they'd come to better understand their brother's ways, for the most part gentle and loving toward all in the family.

But from time to time, his temper was sudden and most often unpredictable. Things others chose to overlook would send Hollis into a tantrum. It was those violent moments that continually reminded the girls and their parents that Hollis wasn't like other 19-year-olds, far from it.

Regardless, Nelson, Charlotte and the twins worked at making each day as routine and manageable as possible; and for the most part they succeeded.

But none of the Vandables could have anticipated the terror that was to visit their home and change their lives in early March, 1878.

oooo

The Legend of Roaring Gorge Gaines

Before squeezing the trigger on the huge 1853 Model Springfield, Felton Baggett tried to marshal his nerve and ignore his pain. He tried to blink his right eye free of distortion, still his breathing and center the metal site in the middle of Vandable's chest.

He whispered words into the stillness of the moment: "Vandable, you ain't gonna live to see that land be yourn or any of them younguns either," his cheek pressed against the left side of the musket's oily, discolored stock.

For Felton Baggett, the agonizing moment ended when the huge rifle detonated and powered its 58-caliber ball across the narrow end of the Gorge. For the Vandables the terror had just begun.

Baggett had always been a good shot, good with both long and hand guns. But that day, the painful cancer devastating his body and the obvious angst of the moment fouled his aim.

He likely never saw whether his efforts found success. He turned and made good his escape while the white smoke still swirled around his head.

As the super-heated ball neared the opposite side, Vandable bent over to reset another piece of oak on the chopping block. The timing and circumstance were critical as the round cleared Vandable's left shoulder by fractions of an inch.

From there it was on line to cut a furrow along the left side of his son's skull, slipping under the scalp before erupting through the skin at the back of the 19-year-old's head.

Knocked backwards, Hollis tumbled twice before scrambling to his feet and running for the woods, screaming and bellowing like a wounded, terrified animal.

Realizing a shot had come from the opposite side of the Gorge; Vandable fell on his stomach, spun on his chest to look over his left shoulder, shouting "Hollis! Hollis! Come back son!"

It was a plea that went unanswered and a moment when the story of the Vandable man began.

Two

The Lay of the Land

Bounds County was sparsely populated in the late 1800's. Fewer than five people per square mile made their home on the hillsides and in the valleys of the Cohutta Wilderness.

Most of the homesteaders worked farms or logged the thick southern pines and towering hardwoods.

Good, flat land was indeed scarce, with randomly rolling hills punctuated by a scattering of peaks and medium-sized, forest-covered ridges.

oooo

But, by far, the area's most prominent landmark was a mile-long, north-south scar cut by the Roaring River through Buzzard Dome Rock Formation in the upper end of the county. The falls at the head of the Gorge and the water it sent tumbling through the ravine heightened the formation's striking topography, while harmonizing and amplifying the voices of wind and water between the quartzite formations and stair-step ledges of its grey-green walls.

For centuries, Roaring Gorge and the river it cradled served to inspire a feeling of majesty, as well as mystery in those who stood at the formation's edge.

Ten miles south of the Gorge, in and around Boundsville, most roads were flat and reasonably well maintained. But shortly after leaving the county seat, with few exceptions, they became little more than uneven, hand-widened wagon and pedestrian trails.

In the late 19th century, the northern end of Bounds County was a rugged environment, requiring its residents maintain an equally-rugged way of life.

Three

The Bounds County Law

The task of enforcing the law in the county's 485 square miles fell to Enoch Eckley. Most of the people in the area knew him as "Major", the rank he'd attained as a relatively young man fighting for the Confederacy.

When Hollis Vandable was shot, Eckley had been Sheriff going on eight years. In that time he'd dealt with everything from trespassing, to disorderly conduct to moonshining.

There was no doubt the county had its share of bootleggers and the like, but someone that would shoot down a neighbor in cold blood was something very different — a crime that quickly became a troublesome challenge for the second term sheriff, as well as his fellow Bounds County residents.

oooo

Eckley was a big man, standing well over six-feet tall. He sported a full, graying beard; wore his pants tucked into knee-high, lace-up boots; and donned a confederate-gray, pin-stripe vest under his three-quarter length, black, tweed coat. The gold star pinned to the front of his Stetson bowler matched-up well with the oversized watch chain that smiled across the front of his chest. There was no holster, only a second chain which ran from his belt to a ring on the handle of the Colt M1889 .38 he carried in his pants pocket.

It's said he'd asked a local seamstress to both deepen and reinforce the pocket, resizing the opening so that the revolver handle was exposed and readily retrievable.

Everyone knew he worked hard at his job. Eckley was just as determined in his efforts to solve crime as he was predictable in his choice of simple, unconventional dress.

oooo

The missing boy's family had been looking for most of the day when Major Eckley rode up. As expected, Sergeant, his large canine partner was not far behind. By early afternoon, Nelson, Charlotte and the twins were emotionally and physically drained. All were clearly relieved to see the veteran lawman rein his horse to a stop, dismount and slip a rope through the metal ring on Sergeant's collar.

The Legend of Roaring Gorge Gaines

If you saw the Sheriff, you could be sure Sergeant wasn't far away.

The 4-year-old, mix-breed pointer had no formal training and didn't carry the credentials of a bloodhound, but his ability to smell, particularly something "out of the ordinary", had proven helpful to his owner on more than a few occasions.

oooo

"Nelson, I'm sorry it took me so long to get here, but I was on the other end of the county when the Wilkins boy found me."

"That's okay Major, I appreciate James lettin' his son go and get you. Somethin' terrible has happen here! That damn Felton Baggett tried to shoot me down this mornin', but hit my boy instead."

"Where's Hollis now?"

"We ain't got the foggiest idea. He ran off into the woods behind the house, and we ain't heard or seen nothin' of him since. You know how he is, Major. There ain't no tellin' how far he'll go or what he'll do. His mama's worried sick. And, I gotta tell ya, I am too."

"I'm sure, Nelson....you say Felton Baggett did the shootin'. How ya know that?"

"'cause the shot came from right across the Gorge and there ain't but one group of folks over there, the Baggetts. And you know how spiteful Felton's been since that judge ruled in my favor! Of course, it was Felton Baggett, shootin' at me, but hittin' my boy," said Vandable, again trying to hide a growing tremble.

The facts were few, and it didn't take Vandable long to summarize what appeared to have happened – his timely move at the woodpile; Hollis standing only a few feet behind; the shot knocking him down and the nineteen-year-old's panicked run for the woods, screaming and flailing his arms.

"Okay, Nelson, let me look around and take a walk back into the woods. Why don't you just sit here and try to relax for a bit," said Eckley, resting his hand on Vandable's right shoulder.

Hollis' father responded with a nod before putting an elbow on each knee and dropping his face into upturned hands.

Charlotte Vandable and the twins, who had been standing nearby, went back to the house to try and rest before Eckley and Sergeant began to walk toward the place where Hollis entered the woods.

oooo

Eckley was well into the trees before Sergeant found the first traces of blood. Hollis appeared to have placed a bloody palm against a hickory tree. In addition, there were several drops on the dry leaves at the base of the large hardwood.

Further down the slope toward one of the streams that spilled over into the ravine, Sergeant began to whine and pull harder on the hemp rope running from Eckley's hand to the leather collar.

At the edge of the water, prints and other sign indicated the boy had knelt, probably trying to wash blood from his head and upper body.

Then came the first time Enoch Eckley heard the echoing sound from further down the Gorge. It was more a howl, a mournful bellow than a shout or yell.

It was an unnerving cry Eckley and others were to hear many times in and around Roaring Gorge.

Four

Felton Baggett's Final Act

While searchers looked for Hollis Vandable, Sheriff Eckley looked for answers.

In the early afternoon on the day of the shooting, Eckley visited the Baggett home. The Sheriff had known the family since he'd first run for office. Major had always found Felton to be a pleasant, albeit somewhat private man, certainly not one you'd readily expect to shoot down a long-time neighbor.

But the fact was, most of the mountain folks in Bounds County and the surrounding area were mum when it came to expressing their deepest feelings. It was something Eckley understood well. Was Felton Baggett capable of cold-blooded murder?

The Sheriff knew he was likely as capable as any strong-willed man who felt deeply wronged – a man who'd come to believe retribution was fully justified.

oooo

"Good morning, Sheriff. Please come in and have a seat," said Beth Baggett as she pointed toward two straight-back chairs.

"Thank you, Mrs. Baggett. That fire does look good."

Major Eckley removed his Stetson bowler and began spinning it between his fingers as he sat down to the left of the fireplace. Mrs. Baggett sat very erect, looking proper in her manner as she focused on the Sheriff's face.

"Beth, I'm here to see your husband. Is he around?"

"He's out in one of the fields right now. I'm not sure just when he'll be back in."

"Okay. If you'd point me in the right direction, I'll just walk out there and we can visit."

There was a moment of silence before Beth Baggett asked the obvious question; "What's this about, Sheriff?"

"I just have a few questions I need to ask Felton."

Mrs. Baggett pressed the matter. "This is a little frightening. Could you please tell me what's wrong. Has something happened? Please tell me."

Enoch Eckley didn't reply immediately. In the 1870's, it was a little unusual for a mountain woman to assert herself in subject matters typically left to the men, especially when the subject matter involved increasingly stern expressions on the face of an imposing, touch-minded lawman.

Behind what was often a somewhat gruff demeanor, Eckley was really more sensitive and empathetic than might be thought. He understood the Baggett woman's concern.

After smiling softly he replied, "Well, I'm afraid there's been a shooting at the Vandable place, and it looks like the shot came from across the Gorge – from somewhere over here near your place, Mrs. Baggett. And I need to talk to Felton about that."

"Oh, my God, Sheriff, was anyone hurt?"

"Yes, the Vandable boy, Hollis, was hit."

"Is he alright?"

"Well…..we don't know right now. He ran off into the woods and so far we ain't been able to find him. Now, could you please head me in the right direction so I can go speak with your husband?"

"Sheriff, surely you don't think Felton would do something like that, do you?"

Eckley didn't answer. He just stood and recalled the issue.

"Ma'am, now please."

"Certainly," replied Felton's wife before standing to show Major Eckley the path through the woods that led to the corn field where she thought her husband had gone.

oooo

Walking through the strip of woods separating the Baggett house from the modestly-sized fields beyond, Eckley instinctively pulled the revolver from his pants pocket to confirm there were no empty chambers in the cylinder.

Sergeant was at his side.

No more than five or six acres across, it was possible to stand on one side of the field and see the other.

At first look, Baggett was nowhere to be seen.

Not until Sergeant took several steps into the field did Eckley take notice. The dog was looking at the trees on the other side of the foot-high cornstalk stubble. His lapped-over ears were standing out from the side of his head and his chest was squared off.

"What is it sarge...what ya see buddy?"

A moment passed before Eckley encouraged the 70-pound pointer across the field. "Go, Sergeant. Check it out now."

Sarge stopped twice, waiting for the Sheriff to catch up. Eckley was in good condition for a man his age, but keeping up with the powerful, bounding hunting dog across six acres of rough ground was asking a little much.

oooo

Having gotten as close as he thought Eckley might want him to get, Sergeant stopped ten feet from the body, turned back to look at Eckley and bark with some urgency.

When the pair reached the spot where Baggett had sat down against the base of a sizable oak tree, a closer look showed Beth's husband started with his left wrist, where two passes hadn't gotten the job done. Moving to the right side of his neck, a deep pass with the straight razor, finished what he'd set out to do. The pearl-handled razor was still held tightly in his right hand.

Baggett's death was only the first of the troubling occurrences to follow the disappearance of Hollis Vandable.

Five

Chester Snelson's Chickens

One puzzling development occurred the day of Felton Baggett's funeral.

Everyone for miles around was at the Boundsville Baptist Church as the door to the Snelson chicken coop was torn from its hinges. The intruder had already rummaged through the three-room farmhouse.

> *Five Days after the Shooting*

When the Snelsons returned from the funeral and discovered the damage they sent for Enoch Eckley.

oooo

"Major, I'm sorry to get you out here this evenin', but I thought you might oughta know 'bout this," said Snelson, directing

Eckley around the corner of the house toward the back yard.

"That's no problem. Let's see what you've got back here."

Both men stopped in front of the coop, looking at the damage, which was clearly extreme.

"Reckon why they didn't just unlatch the door? I mean, why tear things up like that, Sheriff?"

Eckley hesitated before answering. "I don't know, Chester. I don't know why he would nearly pull the door off like that. Maybe he was just in a hurry...afraid you folks might come home and catch him, or it could just be they were plain ol' spiteful."

"...don't think he was afraid of gettin' caught....seems like he would've heard the wagon comin' up the hill on that old rocky road a good bit before we would've seen anyone around here. And there's another reason I say that. Come on down here and take a look at this."

Snelson led Eckley toward the woods.

Sergeant was already in the tree line before the two men walked up. Both watched as the pointer sniffed at the chicken heads, entrails and feathers lying in the dry leaves.

"Whoever took the hens killed and dressed 'em right here. Now, that seems strange to me, Sheriff. They must not've been too afraid of gettin' caught."

"Yeah, Chester, that's strange enough."

oooo

"What'd he do, ring their heads off?" asked Eckley leaning down beside the remains.

"No, no, he cut 'em off. And that's part of somethin' else you might find interestin'. He pulled my new ax out of the choppin' block, cut off the chickens' heads and then it looks like he took the ax with him."

Major looked up at Snelson, for the first time beginning to see more in the situation than had first appeared.

"And, in addition to the ax, whoever it was took the canvas I use to cover the wagon and a roll of rope out of the barn."

And there's more you'll find interestin'. It's really the reason we sent for you. A kitchen drawer was dumped in the floor and Martha says her biggest butcher knife is gone, and so's one of her big, black cookin' pots. They were taken after whoever it was tore the kitchen door down, just like the one there on the coop."

"I mean, we're like other folks around here, Major; we don't lock things up. Why not just unlatch the chicken coop door or simply turn that door knob up at the house. Why rip stuff up and kick things in?"

As he often did when thinking something through, Enoch Eckley was tapping his index fingers and thumbs inside the lower pockets on his vest. Before he could fashion an answer to the question just posed by the Bounds County logger, Chester Snelson expressed a concern that furrowed his brow.

"And, where's Sammy? We ain't seen or heard him since we got home. Sammy!

Come on, you old mutt!" shouted Snelson in a way that implied it was only his latest attempt to call in the rangy dog.

Eckley glanced toward the woods in response to Snelson's calls and whistles for the hound, still turning over in his head pieces of the story he'd heard.

Of course, it wasn't just the missing chickens or on-the-spot slaughtering that really bothered Eckley; it was the angry-looking damage and the assortment of things taken which proved most worrisome.

Typical of his approach, up until that point, Enoch Eckley had done more listening than talking.

His next words came as a question. "You sure that's everything you folks noticed missin'?"

"Well, there was one other thing – the box of matches we keep on the mantle is gone."

Another moment of silence followed before Chester Snelson's frustration showed again.

"I mean....slaughtered chickens, an ax, knife, rope, canvas, a box of matches and things torn all to hell?"

"What ya make of it, Major?"

"Well, I'm not sure right now, Chester…just not sure…maybe somebody's gonna be settin' up housekeepin' out in the woods, and he just don't like the idea," said the Sheriff with a quick smile.

Again, both men looked silently at one another before Eckley decided to send Snelson back up the hill.

"Tell you what, Chester. Why don't you get on back up to the house? I know your wife might be a little upset with what's been goin' on. I think Sarge and I'll walk on back into the woods a little and see what we can see."

It got dark quickly in the narrow valleys of Bounds County. Running up the wick in the lantern, Eckley and Sergeant hurried down the gradual slope behind the Snelson house. There was no more than an hour left before darkness would call the impromptu search to a halt.

The only thing they found before a distant, chilling shriek from the deep woods split the gathering darkness was the hacked and bludgeoned body of an aging hound.

Six

The Bratcher's Barnyard Bedroom

Ben and Rachel Bratcher lived on the eastern side of the Gorge, about two miles

In the Month of June, 1878

south of the Vandable homeplace. As with the Vandable family, the Bratchers worked tobacco, corn and beans on their thirty-plus acres. There were two children, a grown son and a daughter, Pricilla.

The family's four-room farmhouse had always been more than adequate – that was until Ben's older brother, Bud, came to live with the family.

Pricilla's uncle struggled with severe curvature of the spine – a condition that had worsened the final five years of his life. He was loved by all who knew the retired Methodist circuit rider. He was always thoughtful of others. Predictably, he did all he could to make his stay as trouble-free as possible.

Several years before coming to live with Ben and Rachel, he'd lost his wife to the severe, debilitating effects of rheumatoid arthritis. He knew well the challenges faced by family members who live with an acutely handicapped individual.

Before making the move, he'd insisted on helping Ben finish off a storage room on the side of the family's barn. Windows and a door leading to the outhouse were installed, as well as a wood stove and other necessities. He'd refused to inconvenience his brother's family by living in the house itself.

Bud died rather suddenly, living only fifteen months after moving in the room off the barn.

Leaving it pretty much as it was when Bud was alive, Ben and Rachel simply closed it up following his death.

A few weeks after the funeral, it was Pricilla that made the discovery, when she went to the barn bedroom to get coverings off Uncle Bud's mattress. It was early on a

Saturday morning, and the room was still warm, ashes glowing in the stove. The discovery became even more puzzling when she found the bed covers under, not on the bed.

oooo

"How did they get in the room?" asked Eckley as he shook the lock Bratcher had installed on the outside door to Uncle Bud's former sleeping quarters.

"Come around here, and I'll show you."

Both men entered the barn, where Ben moved two loosened boards on the barn wall at the back of the add-on room, revealing a triangular opening through which the intruder gained access.

Judging from all that was found, it was clear that someone had spent a good deal of time inside, building low fires in the stove, using a wash pan to heat a variety of food items and hiding below the bed springs as they retreated from the night.

At that time, there were no specifics as to who it may have been or just how long the intruder or intruders had used Reverend Bratcher's former room. But it grew to become a part of the puzzling story surrounding Hollis Vandable.

There was one definite outcome after word of the Bratcher's visitor made the rounds. Nelson and Charlotte Vandable were greatly encouraged. There was a simple reason the discovery meant more to the Vandable household than anyone else. Nelson, his wife and two daughters were the only ones who knew.

Since being frightened by a bad thunderstorm when he was a small boy, Hollis had often slept under the bed.

Seven

Annamae Glascock's Filly

The Glascock family had lived a mile north of the Vandable place a full five years before Hollis' disappearance. During that time Barton and Celia Glascock had become good friends with Nelson and Charlotte.

Late Summer 1878

The Glascock's boy, Eddie, was two years younger than Hollis, but he'd grown to be the closest thing to a day-in-day-out friend Hollis had known. Eddie's happy-go-lucky ways seemed to have a stabilizing effect on the Vandable's son.

Eddie's sister, Annamae, was thirteen in the late summer of 1878. Although two years younger and noticeably smaller, she got along well with the Vandable twins.

The bond between the two households formed around the similarities in their lifestyle. Nelson and Barton's interest in hunting, fishing and seasonal logging, as well as the parallel nature of the crops they worked, provided a great deal of commonality.

The same was true with Charlotte and Celia when it came to gardening; sewing, canning and church volunteer work.

The five children enjoyed time together, even though their ages ranged from thirteen to nineteen.

oooo

There was, however, one marked difference in the families' interests, the Glascock's love of horses. The eight they fed and housed ranged from two draft animals that pulled plows and drug logs, to a handsome, deep-red Tennessee walker, two chestnut-colored quarter horses, a pair of appaloosas and their newly-arrived colt.

Of course there were the animals you'd expect to find on a Bounds County farm as well – three cows, a pen for eight hogs, a handful of goats, chickens, ducks, two hounds and an aging mule.

Most of the area's homesteaders had a horse for Sunday buggy time and trips into town. What was unusual about Barton Glascock was the number of horses and the specialty breeds he owned.

oooo

By far the most unusual in the Smoky Mountains were the two appaloosas – Pecos and Pepper. Their breed's roots ran deeply into the American west, where they were far more prominent.

Barton bought them off a peddler who'd passed through Boundsville, heading somewhere up in Virginia. The man had no proof of ownership; no knowledge of the horses' history, how they got their names or explanation as to how he'd come by the pair.

[46]

Glascock didn't really care; he loved horses; and he'd never seen anything like the two magnificent, spotted animals.

Barton never became an expert, but he managed to master something of the Appaloosa's history. He could outline the breeds' connection with the Nez Perce Indians and draw a distinction between a 'pinto' and a 'paint' – the later being the correct reference when speaking of Pecos and Pepper.

The pair's special place in the Glascock livestock lineup is what made Pepper's first foal so special. Early on it was clear that the white rump and dark spots contrasting with the rich bay base color was going to be at least as striking as her parent's markings.

The task of naming the filly fell to Annamae, her new owner. Before the filly's birth, Barton promised the new arrival to his daughter.

Annamae went with 'Treasure', saying that's just how she felt about the frisky new addition to the family's barnyard lineup.

At almost five months, Annamae's dad was afraid the filly's continuous nursing was pulling the mare down. Pepper hadn't yet shown signs of irritation with her foal, but the time had come for Treasure to begin eating grain and other solid vegetation.

oooo

"Annamae, now that we're keepin' Treasure in a separate pen from her mother, you'll need to make sure the gate in always locked," said Barton as he helped his daughter down from the middle rail in the corral fence.

"I will Pa. I'll check it for sure every time I go in and out. And I'll get Eddie to help me make sure the gate's always locked."

"We need to keep her away from Pepper, so when she's hungry she'll learn to go for the feed trough rather than her mother. Until Treasure gets used to that she'll be sniffin' around the fence tryin' to find a way back to her mom. She sees that gate standin' the least bit open, and she'll be gone. Understand?"

"Yes sir, I understand."

oooo

On the day it happened, it wasn't Annamae that left the pen gate slightly ajar, it was Eddie.

The timing couldn't have been worse.

That afternoon the family had tied the two adult Appaloosas to the wagon and taken them to a horse show and dinner on the ground when the storm struck. Lightening, thunder and driving rain brought a sudden end to the community center activities, sending folks scattering for home.

When the Glascocks got back to their farm at the uppermost end of the Gorge, Treasure was long gone. The filly, terrorized by the violent storm and unable to get in the barn, had bolted the cover of the woods.

Eddie's blunder was twofold. After feeding Pecos and Pepper's daughter that morning he'd failed to latch the pen gate as well as open the barn's side door so Treasure could find shelter from the weather.

oooo

Two days of searching failed to turn up any trace of the filly. The rain had washed away any trail. Most felt she'd likely fallen victim to predators or fallen to her death in the Gorge.

It was the morning of the third day when Eddie came running into the kitchen. "Treasure's back! Treasure's back!" Indeed she was. The family's reaction was pure celebration.

oooo

The filly finding shelter during one of Bounds County's violent, late-summer storms; managing to avoid packs of wild dogs and large wildcats for more than two days; and ultimately finding her was back to the Glascock yard wasn't inconceivable.

But there was one thing that morning that couldn't be attributed to the young

[51]

horse. Treasure didn't tie herself to that top rail in the barnyard fence. For that no one could be found who would take responsibility.

It was months later that the Glascocks came to believe the filly's safe return was the work of the person whose shrieks and howls filled the deepest woods surrounding Roaring Gorge – a person they'd known as Hollis Vandable.

Eight

Down Near Hen's Egg Boulder

Following the boy's hysterical flight into the forest, Hollis' father routinely walked the edge of the Gorge in hopes of discovering something of his son's fate.

> *Early fall, 1878*

Using brass binoculars borrowed from Sheriff Eckley, Nelson had seen red-tailed hawks, black bears, foxes, and a variety of other wildlife, but nothing of Hollis.

Several months after the shooting organized searches had dwindled to almost nothing, as friends and neighbors chose to concede what seemed obvious – Hollis

Vandable had been forever swallowed up by the thick forests of Bounds County.

But that changed, at least for Hollis' parents, when they learned the details of the Bratcher invasion and the return of Annamae's filly. Nelson increased his forays into the woods, finding an elevated spot from which he could survey the ravine and the surrounding forest.

oooo

In the fall of 1878, there was another development which strengthened the family's hope of finding Hollis alive. But even as it brought encouragement and renewed determination, the event stood challenged by the seemingly impossible.

It had been six months since Felton Baggett's errant shot sent the boy into the woods – six months in which Hollis would have been forced to deal with disorientation brought on by injury, hunger and exposure to the mountains' ragged terrain.

Could Nelson and Charlotte Vandable's son still be alive? It was a relentless question.

At best, it seemed highly unlikely, but not impossible.

oooo

Nelson Vandable used the Civil War-era glasses he'd borrowed from Enoch Eckley to scan the tree lines and ravine floor.

In most places, the craggy walls were too steep and treacherous for anyone to hide. No, if he were going to spot Hollis, it would be above the rim, in the trees, or at the very bottom along the river.

That day in mid-September it wasn't some unexpected movement or flash of reflected sunlight that drew the field glasses to a point perhaps a mile down the river.

It was a shape, a 'something' silhouetted against the gray background of Hen's Egg Boulder.

Vandable shortly convinced himself that someone was sitting on the ground at the point where the narrowing end of the huge, egg-shaped stone slipped back into the bank.

But even with help provided by the wartime optics, the distance and distortion caused by a single, large tree's smattering of leaf growth kept Vandable from gaining an in-focus view of the object near the edge of Roaring River.

Hollis' father lowered the glasses and stood up, thinking and mouthing to himself: *What's…what's that? Could it be…?*

Pulling the binoculars up to his face a second time, he tried to find just the right distance between the worn, leather, eye cups and his eyes. The harder he tried to figure out what he was seeing, the more knotted up and confusing it appeared to be.

A moment or two more and he came to the conclusion logic would dictate: *No. No. It's my eyes playing tricks on me. That's not a person.*

Fighting the notion he should write the sighting off to imagination or the influence of wishful thinking, he almost impulsively moved down the edge of the Gorge in hopes of clearing the distant limbs from his line of sight.

That's when supposition turned into conviction. As he focused on the same spot in the sand just in front of Hen's Egg

Boulder, the object was no longer there. No question, something had been there, but in the time it had taken Nelson Vandable to move fifteen feet on down the rock ledge, it looked to have disappeared back into the undergrowth at the base of the ravine wall.

Hollis' father moved a quarter mile further down the Gorge where the rocky wall was less steep and the footing more dependable.

The better part of an hour was required to reach the large rock. As Vandable alternated hands, one used to hold the binoculars against his chest while the other helped steady his descent, he grew more and more confident that someone had been on the nearside of the famous rock – perhaps Hollis, squatting as close to the boulder as possible.

The Legend of Roaring Gorge Gaines

 oooo

Standing only feet from the place where he felt sure the person had been, Vandable struggled with disappointment.

Unlike the clear evidence at the Snelson and Bratcher farms, there was nothing at Hen's Egg to confirm someone having been there.

And yet, that day, there were two more things to help keep the family's hope alive: Nelson's determined reliance on what he'd seen and the shrill scream he heard while climbing back out of Roaring Gorge.

oooo

Enoch Eckley had told the Vandables about the strange cries from the woods, but it was the first time Nelson had heard them from himself. He found the cries and bellows unsettling to hear, but even more confirmation that Hollis was alive.

Someone was out there, hiding and growing more accustomed to the thick forest. An injured boy was becoming The Vandable Man.

Nine

The Pumpkin Tradition

Hollis' father was a man of faith and conviction — a religious man, whose beliefs were instrumental in getting him through the months following the disappearance of his

> *Eight Months after the Shooting*

son. He and Charlotte prayed daily for their boy's safe return, and the Thanksgiving holiday, 1878, was certainly no exception.

After the large roasting hen and several traditional dishes were placed on the table, the family gathered 'round and joined hands.

"Oh God, we give thanks for all our blessings — our good health, this warm house and the bounty of our fields. Charlotte and I thank you for our girls

and the joy they bring into our home. We also pray that you would continue to watch over Hollis, wherever he may be, and should it be your will, please deliver him back to us, where he is so greatly missed and deeply loved. Amen."

"Thank you, Nelson," whispered his wife as she squeezed her husband's hand. Rebecca and Bonnie smiled softly at their parents. They knew how difficult the past months had been.

Of course both girls missed their brother greatly, but the whimsical ways of the young helped them escape the daily parental pain felt by Nelson and Charlotte as they dealt with the unknown.

The family's hope for Hollis' return wasn't completely gone, but each passing day seemed to render the possibility more unlikely.

The Legend of Roaring Gorge

Gaines

oooo

Eight months after the shooting, life within the Vandable household had begun to slip into a simpler, less-stressful routine – one without Hollis and the day-to-day challenges his condition presented. But each time the Vandables began to accept the increasing likelihood he was gone forever, something happened that further flew in the face of reason, something like the unexpected discovery the morning after Thanksgiving.

There were no classes in the one-room school house on Thanksgiving Friday. They weren't scheduled to resume until the following Tuesday. But school or no school, there was no break in the twins' pre-dawn chores.

Among other things, Rebecca and Bonnie were charged with milking the two cows their father kept on the farm.

oooo

"Race you to the barn!" shouted Rebecca as she sprinted out to a head start on her sister.

"Wait a minute, 'becca, that's not fair," replied Bonnie as she struggled to overcome her sister's quick advantage. Both laughed and enjoyed the moment, just as they'd done on so many mornings before the family tragedy.

The girls were tall and athletically built. They were good workers, having grown up helping their father with many tasks on the farm, some quite demanding such as clearing fields and the associated logging.

oooo

[64]

"Bonnie, you wanta milk Queen or Daisy," asked Rebecca as each girl picked up a stool and headed for the stalls.

"I'll take Daisy this mornin', since I had that run-in with Queen yesterday."

Queen, the older and more cantankerous of the two, often seemed to look for ways to make things difficult, regardless of who was sitting on the milking stool. On Thanksgiving morning, Queen had twice driven her right, rear hoof into the ground only inches from Bonnie's foot. Every other day was about all either girl wanted to tangle with the large brown and white cow.

oooo

Milk covered the bottom of both pails before either of the girls spoke. They were thinking about Hollis and how much he enjoyed going with them to the barn at

[65]

milking time. When he wasn't sitting on a stool squeezing a stream of milk into a pail, he would sit overhead at the edge of the loft floor, swinging his legs and watching his sisters. Hollis clearly enjoyed being around the girls whenever possible.

Rebecca and Bonnie tried not to talk about it a great deal, but Hollis was often on their minds, particularly when doing something in which he'd been a regular companion.

"'becca, what do you think happened to Hollis?"

Following a brief pause to consider her response, Rebecca seemed anxious to cut the exchange short; "Oh, I don't know, Bonnie."

"You, think he's dead?"

"I think we shouldn't talk about it. It won't help. That's what I think! If he's gone, he's gone, and there's nothin' we can do about it," replied Rebecca, sounding as though she may well have overcome more of the uncertainty surrounding Hollis' disappearance than had her sister.

Expressing what sounded like an afterthought, Rebecca pickup up the subject again. "The woods, the Gorge and that river are dangerous places. Hurt like he was, it's hard to think he could still be alive. I don't like thinkin' and talkin' about it…makes me sad."

Several moments passed before Bonnie responded. Even as close as the girls were, each seemed to chose their words with care when talking about what had happened and the trauma it had brought into the family.

"I know. It does me too. But I heard Ma and Pa talkin' again last night about someone stealin' things at the Snelson farm, and Pa seeing that person down by the river. How do you explain those things, especially the part about someone sleeping under the Bratcher's bed? We both know how Hollis used to do that when he was here."

Rebecca was troubled by the subject, determined to keep it from shaping her thoughts for the rest of the day.

"Bonnie that was a long time ago!"

There was another period of silence before Rebecca spoke up again.

"How did he get over his injuries; how'd he keep from bleedin' to death; what's he been eatin'; what's he done about something to wear; and where's he been livin' and sleepin' all this time?" countered Rebecca, fashioning her rebuttal in the form of several thorny questions – questions she'd heard her parents pose.

As in previous times, when the girls talked about the lingering uncertainties following Felton Baggett's shot across the Gorge, the discussion ended abruptly, without the satisfaction of even a few answers.

As usual, the twins finished milking at the same time, before replacing the stools by the front wall.

After pulling the barn doors closed and heading for the back porch, they saw them, three smaller ones sitting around a larger one, the largest representing their parents and one each for the three Vandable children.

As was the case each year, they were in the center of the table on the landing, right where they were always put to await cleaning and use in one of Hollis' favorites – pumpkin pie.

Someone with a clear message in mind had gone the extra mile to seek out and deliver the bright orange fruit, someone to whom the holiday tradition was especially meaningful. That fall, Nelson Vandable hadn't planted pumpkins.

Ten

As Interest Waned

Most Bounds County residents were aware of what happened on the Vandable farm, as well as the puzzling events that followed. For months after the shooting, many remained intrigued.

Early February, 1879

However, as the holidays passed and 1879 rolled around, folks in the area found it less and less credible that Hollis Vandable could have overcome the injuries described by his father and survived that year's unusually-cold Cohutta winter.

As the months passed, even the facts surrounding the Snelson and Bratcher intrusions seemed to lend little credence to the notion that a mentally-challenged 19-year-old could be living somewhere in the woods. By the spring of 1879, there was little discussion about the mystery surrounding Hollis Vandable.

What interest remained was the result of Nelson Vandable's persistent efforts toward keeping the subject alive and promoting the need for additional searches.

The person he tried hardest to convince was Sheriff Eckley. Credibility the well-respected officer would bring to any further organized search was something the Vandable family sought on a regular basis.

But the fact was, a full year after the shot was taken, the Sheriff's thinking had become more like the growing number of skeptics around town.

oooo

"Now Major, look at what's happened since March of last year….the break-in at Chester Snelson's place and the wilderness-survival things taken? Hollis was slow-witted, but he understood the woods and knew the basics it would take to live there."

Major Eckley sat at his desk, reared back in the squeaky wooden chair, just as he'd done many times before, listening to Nelson Vandable argue the point that the mystery surrounding Hollis wasn't just a curiosity, but a tragic story of a missing boy whose fate must be determined.

Eckley didn't respond at that point, as he continued to tap the tips of his index fingers against his thumbs in each lower vest pocket.

As he'd done often before, Vandable resumed his argument.

"Major, how likely is it that someone other than Hollis would set up a hidden entrance into the Bratchers' barn bedroom and sleep under the bed...for God's sake....just like he used to do at home when he was frightened?"

"And what about the person I saw down by the river near Hen's Egg Boulder, I didn't imagine that. And then there's them pumpkins bein' left on the back stoop, set up just like Hollis did every year?"

oooo

Eckley leaned forward, placing his elbows back on the desk top.

"Nelson, there ain't one bit of proof that Hollis is the one that stole them things from Chester Snelson's place; and I'll admit it does look strange, with someone sleepin' under the bed and all, but I ain't found nothin' to argue Hollis was the one in the Bratcher's bedroom. Maybe he was, but there ain't a thing to justify folks headin' off into the woods for the umpteenth time."

"And, when it comes to somebody squattin' down at Hen's Egg, you yourself said there weren't footprints or nothin' else in them rocks to confirm anyone bein' there!"

"Nelson, sometimes our eyes see what we want 'em to see. Ya know?"

[75]

"Well....what about them pumpkins bein' left on that table just like Hollis always used to do? Who else would know to do such a thing? It just had to be Hollis!"

"Nelson, not another person has confirmed knowing about Hollis doin' that every Thanksgivin'. Just like the Hen's Egg thing, the only folks that can confirm the pumpkins most likely comin' from Hollis are you folks, and nobody wants Hollis to be alive more than you and your family."

What Eckley was implying came through loud and clear. Then, the big lawman smiled at his friend, before tilting his head to the right in a gesture of understanding.

"I'm sorry, Nelson. After all these months and what looks like an end several months back to the clues you been talkin' about, I'm just not in a position to launch another big search around here by the same people who've searched these woods five or six times before. I'm sorry."

oooo

After Vandable left, Eckley slumped back in his chair, for the first time knowing he'd been less than honest with someone asking for his help.

Although he'd been able to move the Vandable issue pretty much to the back of his daily agenda, the boy and his family continued to cross Enoch Eckley's mind daily. It was the biggest puzzle he'd faced since taking office.

oooo

Major glanced at Sarge who was looking hard from his bed in the far corner. Over time the pointer had developed a sense which told him when Eckley was troubled. The Sheriff replied to his dog's stare with a question.

"You think I shoulda told him, do ya?"

Sergeant's response was soft and simple. He slowly lowered his head back to his right forearm.

What troubled the Sheriff was simple.

He'd elected not to mention the random number of farm animals that had gone missing, along with men's shirts and pants taken from area clothes lines over the past six months. Nor did he mention the three peeping tom complaints from area farms.

PP

Eleven

The Swinford-Tuckerman Wedding

———✦———

Things took a real turn just over a year after the shooting – a turn that not only rekindled the interest of Enoch Eckley, but most people in the area.

> *In the Summer of 1879*

The occasion was the Tuckerman-Swinford wedding, a simple but elegant-for-the-day ceremony involving two of Bounds County's most prominent families. The Tuckermans were successful farmers and merchants, and the Swinfords owned a large sawmill operation south of Boundsville.

All had gone well as the flower-covered buggy left the church amid shouts of best wishes from those in attendance. But as the legend goes, the festive atmosphere was to come to an abrupt end under disturbing circumstances.

A mile or so from the church, Margret was the first to hear the grunts and hard breathing from behind the buggy. The blurred view available through the cheap, distorted glass in the rear, oval window offered little by way of explanation.

Not until the new bride leaned around the right front upright of the overhead cover did she see the broad outline of a man, running in a slightly crouched-over position, sleeveless arms pumping, as he chased the young couple up the slight hill in the middle of the road.

Shortly after leaving the church for his father's Gorge-side hunting cabin, Preston Swinford had put the big mare in a shallow trot. If he hadn't, the pursuer would likely have already overtaken the newlyweds.

oooo

"Oh God, Preston, someone is chasing us!"

Swinford stood in the front floorboard and looked back over the top of the buggy, and there it was – a stocky, strange, hunkered-over form struggling to catch up in the fading evening light.

There was nothing being shouted, nothing thrown, no specific physical threat, only the grunts, unusually heavy breathing and intermittent wails that reminded Swinford of someone crying.

Two slaps across the horse's rump with the heavy reins accompanied by three shrill whistles and the buggy began to pull away.

Perhaps the most unnerving moment came after the powerful mare had been in a strong gallop for some good distance, and Swinford realized the figure had indeed fallen back, but was still coming.

Not until the buggy and its occupants neared the Swinford cabin and the intruder was no longer in sight did the mournful howl come from the woods on the Gorge-side of Boundsville Road.

The Legend of Roaring Gorge
Gaines

oooo

Another shock awaited the Swinfords after Preston's near-frantic efforts succeeded in unlocking the front door. Shutters on a rear window had been ripped off and the cabin interior ransacked.

Most notable among the things missing were two rifles, a shotgun, appropriate ammunition, and several bottles of Mr. Swinford's prime whiskey.

The mare had little time to rest before she was again pressed into action, pulling the bride and groom back toward Boundsville through the thickening darkness.

According to fully-committed students of the legend, the strangest part of the entire wedding-night account may have been the particularly-eerie return of the couple's tormentor – only heard and not seen, as he crashed through the darkened woods alongside the fleeing buggy. It was then that Swinford was sure the sounds he was hearing were more akin to wails and crying than anything else.

oooo

The troubling events following the Swinford-Tuckerman wedding did two things.

First, they transformed random local conversations about a boy tragically lost in the wilderness into fearful and wide-spread talk about the 'wild man in the woods'.

And secondly, they left Enoch Eckley with two considerations – who had chased and frightened the young bride and groom, and who had broken into the Swinford hunting cabin, pillaging and damaging almost everything in sight?

Eckley, like most, quickly developed a two-pronged theory: the two were connected and the culprit was likely an older and bolder Hollis Vandable.

Two days later, as he listened to the Swinfords' description, even Nelson Vandable could see how the heavy-set, long-haired, awkward-looking person might be his missing son. Although he didn't tell Eckley, he remembered how Hollis used to grunt and groan noticeably when running or doing heavy, manual labor.

As for the crying, Vandable also knew Hollis was subject to get very emotional when things he cared about deeply didn't go his way.

It was still a stretch for Eckley, but he was growing more and more willing to concede that Hollis Vandable might still be alive and up to creepy mischief like frightening newlyweds.

But when it came to blaming him for breaking into the Swinford cabin and trashing the place, he remained skeptical.

oooo

It was William Swinford's third visit to the office, wanting to know what progress had been made in the investigation. Preston's father was an influential man and Enoch Eckley had an election coming up. The Sheriff wanted to assure the elder Swinford that all was being done to resolve the matter, but he wasn't going to abandon his growing convictions about responsibility.

"What about this wild man people been talkin' about – Nelson Vandable's youngun that got shot and run off to live in the woods like an animal? Maybe we oughta be lookin' for him, Sheriff....next time he might be able to get his hands on somebody," said Swinford, clearly looking for agreement from the Sheriff.

"Mr. Swinford, it mighta been Hollis Vandable that chased that buggy, but I don't think it was him that tore ya place up."

"And why's that?"

"Well, we've seen things from time to time where it looked like the missing boy might have been involved, but there ain't been no real meanness. Your place was really messed up...in a way that looks to me like whoever did it had a sho 'nough mean streak."

"You had guns taken, and as you may have heard, the Vandable boy was dim-witted and very afraid of loud noises. He didn't like guns. Word is, he steered way clear of 'em."

Preston Swinford's father sat quietly in the chair across from Eckley as the Sheriff continued with his reasoning.

"Then there's the liquor that ya boy said went missin'. Unless he's developed a sudden taste for brown whiskey while living out there in the woods, it don't seem like that helps make the case for Hollis Vandable bein' the one that broke in. There's a few folks in Bounds County that might go for long guns, whiskey and the like, but I don't believe that boy's one of 'em."

oooo

Something else supported Eckley's two-perpetrator theory. Sergeant had been unable to detect even the slightest trace of Vandable in the cabin, a scent he'd come to know well the first six months after the boy went missing.

It was then that Eckley began to suspect someone else was in the woods.

Twelve
The Darkest Days Begin

Little seems to have been known about Ben and Venetta Weppler – either that or the old timers must have lost a fair amount as they passed down the Roaring Gorge story.

It's known they came to Bounds County from somewhere in South Carolina to care for Venetta's elderly mother. Her father had died suddenly on the farm.

August of 1879

Venetta's mother passed away shortly after she and Ben settled in. The couple decided to stay rather than return to the low country. Ben had gotten a supervisory job in the area's only textile operation, and Venetta worked as a housekeeper for the textile mill owner.

The Wepplers weren't wealthy people, but they must've made a practice of saving routinely. They were able to buy one of the nicer, white, frame houses just off Main Street in Boundsville.

The above-average house was where it happened – a crime like no one in Bounds County could remember ever happening before. It certainly must have been one of the worst things Enoch Eckley faced during his time in office.

oooo

"I'm gonna be out back," shouted Ben as he went through the screen door, crossed the porch and headed for the garden.

"Okay," replied Venetta from her large, handmade rocking chair in the sitting room.

That's where the attractive, middle-aged homemaker often sat when crocheting, a pastime she greatly enjoyed. Her works not only adorned the Weppler home, but served

[91]

as personal and greatly-appreciated gifts to family and friends on special occasions.

Said to have been involved in a variety of community functions, the Wepplers were well-liked in Boundsville. Their gracious and cordial ways made what happened on that weekday afternoon all the more difficult to take.

oooo

"With the only thing messed up in the room being that turned-over rocker over yonder, it looks like he might've just walked right through the front door, surprised and grabbed hold of Mrs. Weppler, drug her up those stairs, and did what he wanted to do," said Eckley to the Deputy Marshal he'd requested help with the investigation.

Both officers had already been up to the bedroom and seen where the killer brutalized his victim in a variety of grisly ways before stuffing her body under the bed.

Eckley and the marshal moved from the sitting room back to the kitchen, where Ben Weppler's body lay crumpled beside the kitchen table.

Both felt he'd either heard something and returned to the house or simply walked in the back door and encountered the killer at the wash basin. It looked as though he'd been there washing his hands under the sizeable hand pump.

"Sheriff, reckon he just ripped that metal handle right off the back of the pump with his bare hands?" ask the federal man.

"Shore looks like it, don't it," replied Eckley, leaning over again for another look at Weppler's head and the pump handle used to bludgeon the textile mill supervisor

Nothing was taken by the intruder but a bone-handled .38 revolver and the lives of Ben and Venetta Weppler.

oooo

Again, many in the community were ready to blame Nelson and Charlotte Vandable's son for the horrific deed.

But, as with the destructive break-in at William Swinford's place, the law wasn't sure the person folks had begun to call "The Vandable Man" was the guilty party.

Eckley certainly felt reports of someone running through or hiding in the woods were more correctly attributable to Hollis Vandable than the bloody killing of Ben and Venetta Weppler – a mystery that was never resolved, at least not directly.

Thirteen

The Sweeney Tragedy

———•————

Dark days in Bounds County, GA continued into the winter of 1879, with another crime both chilling and equally rare for the simple, family-centered lifestyle of the times.

Third Week of December, 1879

The Legend of Roaring Gorge
Gaines

Not as bloody as what befell the Wepplers, Sara Sweeney's fate was no less shocking to God-fearing people living around Roaring Gorge.

The Dewitt Sweeney family lived on the western side of the Gorge near the southern end of the ravine. He and his wife, Victoria, had Sara late in life. She was their only child.

Victoria's invalid mother and older, bachelor brother lived just south of Dewitt's place. Even at 17-years-of-age, Sara continued to spend a good deal of time with her grandmother, who'd helped Sara pick up her gardening skills.

oooo

The first time he saw her walking home from her grandmother's house, it was by chance. But in the several weeks that followed, he often watched as she passed the old tobacco barn.

Looking through a foot-long hole where mud filler had fallen from between two of the walls' rotting logs, he'd grown enamored of the young woman with the long, blonde hair.

As with Venetta Weppler, infatuation had morphed into something much worse, something that would again bring numbing horror to Bounds County in the second half of 1879.

oooo

Only a quarter mile separated the home of Dewitt Sweeney from the four-room house where Victoria's mother lived. The two houses were connected by West Ridge Road, little more than a wagon path that ran down the west side of the ravine.

The Legend of Roaring Gorge
Gaines

The road separated the yawning Gorge from the surrounding woods and random fields where locals worked their crops.

In years past, Sara's grandmother was often in her flowerbeds and able to keep an eye on her granddaughter as she came to visit or as she returned home. But in recent months Victoria's mother had been unable to do so. A couple of weeks before Christmas, the only eyes to follow Sara's trips back and forth did so with no tenderness or caring.

It was the increased number of trips bringing her ailing grandmother's evening meals that really caught his attention. Most often near dark, he could count on Sara making the trip to her grandmother's place.

He would bend over in the back corner of the dilapidated tobacco barn and step in a half-circle to the left or right, never once shifting his gaze from his slender, green-eyed target.

As with Venetta Weppler, he'd thought repeatedly about when and how he would act out his fantasies. But in the end, there was no real plan, certainly no what-ifs should this or that go wrong. Like most attackers of the innocent, his violence would reflect moments of darting impulse and deeply personal violation.

oooo

"Sara, it's gettin' dark now. As soon as you give granny this, you come right back home," said Mrs. Sweeney, handing the large Mason jar of vegetable soup to her daughter.

"I will, mom. I'll be right back."

As she got to the road, Sara checked to make sure the lid was tight and the jar was sitting in the middle of the cloth her mother had placed around the bottom of the hot jar.

Moving at a brisk pace, she looked down at her feet, watching as only the second pair of new shoes she'd ever owned crunched and scattered small pebbles. Her dad had picked up the black, Sears & Roebuck oxfords a few days earlier at the small post office Terrell Smith operated in the front room of his house.

Sara was anxious to get the soup to her grandmother and again hear the greeting she'd heard so often before – "Oh, it's my beautiful Goldilocks".

oooo

Unlike the other times he'd concentrated on not being seen while peering between the logs, that late afternoon he stood just inside the curing barn door, which he'd left partially open. Just as he'd bolted in to shock and grab Mrs. Weppler, it was his intention to suddenly charge and subdue Sara Sweeney.

In a strangely-exaggerated manner, he was grinding his teeth again — just as he'd always done when having bad thoughts.

oooo

In an instant, Sara was gone, muffled and overpowered by strong hands and the worst of compulsions. All that remained near the tobacco barn was a broken green jar and a single, everyday oxford.

In the span of mere months, the warm, secure feelings of community shared by residents of Boundsville were again shaken to the core.

Fourteen

Questions and Answers

In dealing with the Swinford break-in,
the Weppler killings and the disappearance
of Sara Sweeney, there was little for Eckley
and others to go on.

Of course in 1879 there was no forensics or other tools to assist law enforcement at the cellular level.

All officers had to work with were eyewitness accounts, the potential for obvious evidence at the scene and basic gut instinct developed over years of investigative work.

Using all at his disposal, Eckley was able to discover only a minimal number of leads. He failed to find any trace of Sara Sweeney until well into the winter.

In March, 1880, two years after the shooting that sent the Vandable Man into the woods, and three months after the abduction, hunters made a discovery that answered some question, while raising others.

The Legend of Roaring Gorge
Gaines

When the year's unusually heavy snow melted, what remained of Sara's nude body was found not far from where she had been taken.

But things were complicated by the discovery of the partially-clothed body of a man mere yard from that of the missing young woman.

Examiners weren't able to positively confirm their suspicions, but from tracks and damage to the skeletal remains it appeared he'd been dragged away from Sara Sweeney's body and hacked to death with an ax or large hatchet.

Who was he, and who killed him?

Fifteen
And Finally

——◆——

It was weeks before Enoch Eckley was able to confirm identity of the body in the woods. It was a middle-aged man named Norvell Crogan. He'd gotten a job in a Bounds County warehouse not long after escaping from prison in Rutherford County, Tennessee before becoming Enoch Eckley's 'other man in the woods'.

Beyond that, there are only a few other things to add, each with their own implications:

….long guns, a bone-handled .38 and other stolen items found in the room where Crogan was staying tied him to several crimes in the area;

….a small cave was ultimately located which appeared to have been lived in….near Hen's Egg Boulder;

….of particular interest is the fact that Hollis had been enamored with Sara Sweeney for years, calling her his "only sweetheart";

….reports of someone sleeping under buildings, milk being stolen from buckets suspended in deep cold wells, men's clothing taken from backyard clothes lines, and mournful howls from the woods continued into the early 1880's.

oooo

Today, the majority of young people living in or near the Cohutta Wilderness are unfamiliar with *The Legend of Roaring Gorge*. Many of those who are, simply write it off as far-fetched and fanciful.

But for some the fascination continues, particularly among those who've had occasion to stand at the bewitching edge of Roaring Gorge.

———··———

Ron's other books include:

Stories from Kaston Creek
A collection of southern, depression-era short stories

Elvin Bodner's Stand
A thriller set in a coastal Carolina hunting preserve

Deep Woods Odyssey

The Legend of Roaring Gorge Gaines

An adventure story featuring true-to-their-nature interactions between large, humanized predators

<u>10-8</u>
A collection of police stories based on actual events

<u>The Knotty Pine Murders</u>
A 19th century thriller set in the Great Smoky Mts.